THE LAST KNIGHT
An introduction to Don Quixote
by Miguel De Cervantes
by
Will Eisner
NBM
NANTIER · BEALL · MINOUSTCHINE
Publishing inc.
new york

Also by Will Eisner:
Moby Dick, $15.95 hc, $7.95 pb
The Princess & the Frog, $15.95 hc, $7.95 pb
Sundiata, $15.95 hc, $7.95 pb
($3 P&H 1st item, $1 each addt'l)

We have over 200 graphic novels in stock, ask for our color catalog:
NBM, dept. S
555 8th Ave., Suite 1202
New York, NY 10018
www.nbmpublishing.com/tales

ISBN-10: 1-56163-251-1 hc
ISBN-13: 978-1-56163-251-0 hc
ISBN-10: 1-56163-253-8 pb
ISBN-13: 978-1-56163-253-4 pb
Library of Congress Catalog Card: 00131444
Printed in China

A signed deluxe edition limited to 300 was made of this book.

5 4 3

THE LAST KNIGHT
BY Will Eisner
YOU ARE ALWAYS DREAMING SANCHO!
IN SPAIN... A LONG TIME AGO...
I DREAM OF A TIME WHEN I WAS YOUNG-- MANY YEARS AGO!! A TIME WHEN I WAS HONORED TO KNOW A KNIGHT!
IN MY VILLAGE OF LAMANCHA LIVED ALANZO QUIXANO WHO READ ONLY OLD BOOKS ON CHIVALRY AND KNIGHTHOOD.
ALANZO YOU SPEND ALL YOUR LIFE READING!
ALANZO, IT IS SUPPER TIME!
HA! CHARGE THE DRAGON, SIR KNIGHT!!
3

AH!
BRAVO!
YOU NEITHER EAT NOR SLEEP!
PLEASE, AS HIS OLD FRIENDS ...REASON WITH HIM!!
QUIXANO, QUIXANO! KNIGHTHOOD IS LONG OVER!
BESIDE, YOU ARE TOO OLD FOR SUCH DREAMS
GREAT DEEDS COME FROM GREAT DREAMS!

FOR DAYS QUIXANO POLISHED HIS GREAT GRANDFATHER'S RUSTY OLD SUIT OF ARMOR.

UNTIL AT LAST...

I NOW NEED TO HAVE MYSELF MADE A PROPER KNIGHT!
HO! GET ME THE LORD OF THIS CASTLE!
INN
CASTLE?? HA HA HE MUST BE CRAZY!
THERE HE IS...HA, HA!...HE..HE WANTS THE OWNER!
BUT, BUT!
?
I WISH YOU TO DUB ME A KNIGHT, SIR!
...BUT I'M ONLY A SIMPLE INN-KEEPER!
SHH... HE THINKS YOU ARE THE LORD OF THIS... ER... CASTLE... DON'T ARGUE!
VERY WELL... I DUB THEE... DON QUIXOTE, ...A KNIGHT!
...AND SO THERE RODE OUT OF LAMANCHA THE LAST OF THE GREAT KNIGHTS

I AM DON QUIXOTE DE LA MANCHA A DEFENDER OF OPPRESSED!
OHO! WHAT IS THAT?
OW! OW!
SOUNDS LIKE A PERSON IN NEED OF MY HELP!
FASTER MY DEAR ROSINETTE WE RIDE TO THE RESCUE!
@#!!
HALT!
HALT! I SAY OR I'LL RUN YOU THRU!
?!
?

LISTEN! THIS THIEF HAS BEEN STEALING MY SHEEP!
HE'S BUT A BOY... UNTIE HIM I, DON QUIXOTE ORDER IT!
YES, YES NOBLE SIR!
GO IN PEACE MY BOY!
NOT-SO-FAST BOY!
SO... MY FIRST NOBLE DEED! AND NOW I MUST FIND A FITTING LADY LOVE!

A TRUE KNIGHT MUST HAVE A LADY LOVE!
ONE TO WHOM ONE CAN DEDICATE A DEED OF VALOR!
I NAME YOU DULCINEA DE TOBASCO!
?
AH, YOUR SCARF!
HEY, YOU WANT TO BUY MY SALT PORK? ...I MAKE IT GOOD!
A TOKEN DEAR LADY... TO FLOURISH AND TO HONOR YOUR NAME!
?
HE DIDN'T EVEN TRY MY SALT PORK!

HEY...LOOK! WHAT IS THAT?? HA, HA, HA?
A KNIGHT IN ARMOR!
I CAN'T BELIEVE MY OWN EYES!! HA, HA.
SHH...HE'S COMING AT US!
BRIGANDS! IN THE NAME OF FAIR DULCINEA I ATTACK!
HUH!?
STAND AND FIGHT!
?!
LET ME AT HIM! GRRRR

COME ON... LEAVE HIM.... WE BEST BE ON OUR WAY!
CRAZY NUT!
LATER THAT EVENING IN A GROVE
♪♪♪
WHAT THE... I HEAR SOMEONE SINGING!
?
AHHH♪ FAIR ♪DULCINEA DO YOU♪ WEEP FOR THE TRIALS OF YOUR KNIGHT!

ALONZO IT'S ME SANCHO PANZA OF YOUR VILLAGE!
OOH...I WAS ATTACKED BY A HUNDRED SAVAGES! ...I AM DON QUIXOTE!
YES, YES, YES! HERE NOW LET ME TAKE YOU HOME
AH, SANCHO, YOU SHALL BE MY FAITHFUL SQUIRE!
AND THE NEXT MORNING
'MORNING SIRE... WHAT ARE YOU DOING?
I WILL NOT BE STOPPED. I WILL PURSUE MY QUEST. COME!
BUT WHERE ARE WE GOING?
ON THE ROAD TO FIND WRONGS-TO-RIGHT!
OHO! LOOK THERE A DRAGON ABROAD!
STAND ASIDE SANCHO I WILL DEAL WITH IT!
BUT IT IS ONLY A WINDMILL SIRE

I ATTACK!
YEOW!
HERE, LET ME HELP YOU DOWN SIRE!
OHO... WHAT A FIGHT... UGH, I LOST MY LANCE!
I TOLD YOU IT WAS ONLY A WINDMILL SIRE!
STOP THIS COACH, DRIVER!
YES M'LADY.
WHAT IS THAT?
IT APPEARS TO BE A-A-KNIGHT IN HA HA ARMOR M'LADY.

WHO ARE YOU SIR?!
HE IS DON QUIXOTE DE LA MANCHA!
AT YOUR SERVICE M'LADY ...IN THE NAME OF KNIGHTHOOD!
...AWAY YOU OLD FOOL. YOU ANNOY THE DUCHESS!
OH, HO!
MY SWORD!
MY SWORD!

... WHERE IS HE ?
... WHERE IS HE ??
RIGHT BEHIND YOU, SIRE.
NO, NO, PLEASE SPARE HIM!
I HAVE YOU KNAVE!
BRAVO
... I'VE SPARED YOUR MAN... NOW, I ASK THAT YOU TELL THE KING OF MY VALOR!
OF COURSE I WILL!
CRAZY OLD FOOL!
HA, HA... BUT HE DID BEAT YOU IN FAIR COMBAT!
THAT WAS VERY BRAVE MY LORD.
AH SANCHO, BRAVERY IS THE HEART OF TRUE KNIGHTHOOD! LOOK!
DUST CLOUDS! AN ARMY IN BATTLE! ... COME... WE MUST JOIN IN, SANCHO!
15

LOOK AT THOSE HORSEMEN COMING AT US!
THEY ARE ATTACKING OUR SHEEP!!
A KNIGHT IN ARMOR, ...I DON'T BELIEVE THIS!!
WE MUST STOP HIM!
STONE THE OLD FOOL!
BUT, SIRE THESE ARE ONLY SHEEP.
GETHIM!
LOOK OUT! THOSE SHEPHERDS ARE STONING US!!!
THIS IS NOT A WAY TO TREAT A KNIGHT!!

LET'S GET GOING, BOYS! WE TAUGHT THE OLD FOOL A LESSON.
UGH! THOSE SHEPHERDS NEAR-KILLED YOU!
NO MATTER SANCHO... WE'LL REST IN THIS GLEN TONIGHT...
SIRE, I AM BUT A SIMPLE MAN. EXPLAIN TO ME THE GREAT WAYS OF KNIGHTHOOD...
SANCHO, WE ARE WHAT WE BELIEVE WE ARE... THUS, I AM A KNIGHT BECAUSE I BELIEVE I AM.
IT'S SIMPLE ENOUGH SIRE
AND SO I DO GOOD DEEDS AS ALL KNIGHTS DO.... YAWWNn
YES... ZZZZZz
ARISE, SANCHO! IT IS MORNING AND GREAT ADVENTURES AWAIT US!

AND THERE COMES OUR NEXT ADVENTURE.
I DIDN'T HAVE ANY BREAKFAST, SIRE!
ADVENTURE DOESN'T WAIT ON BREAKFAST, SANCHO!
HALT!
MOVE ALONG JAILBIRDS MOVE, MOVE!
THE BEAST!
SHHH THE GUARD WILL BEAT US.
HALT, I SAY!!
?
BY WHOSE ORDER DO YOU KEEP THESE POOR MEN IN CHAINS, SIR??
THEY'RE THIEVES, CONVICTS!!
I HAVE MY ORDERS FROM THE KING.. NOW, STAND ASIDE, I SAY!
NO SIR!

MY POOR MEN... WHAT WAS YOUR CRIME?
I WAS IN LOVE WITH THE DUKE'S DAUGHTER, SO HE SENT ME TO JAIL!
I WAS TOO POOR TO PAY RENT SO THEY SENT ME TO JAIL FOR LIFE
I SANG TOO LOUD IN THE TOWN SQUARE!
SIGH
STAND ASIDE YOU MEDDLING OLD FOOL... I'LL CUT YOU DOWN!
BOYS LET'S US PUSH THE GUARD OFF HIS HORSE!
QUICK WHILE HE'S BUSY!
WHERE ARE YOU... VILLAIN!
HA I HAVE YOU SIR!
HOORAH

UNCHAIN THOSE POOR SOULS, SANCHO
OH SUCH A NOBLE MAN!
THERE.... YOU ARE FREE!
GO IN PEACE MEN... BUT BE SURE TO TELL THE WORLD OF MY VALOR!
WHAT VALOR? WE SAVED YOU!
YOU OLD FAKE HAW HAW HAW
WE UNSEATED THE GUARD FOR YOU!
YOU OLD FRAUD !!!
LET ME AT HIM !!
COME ON, BOYS, LET'S GO! ...ESCAPE!

OOH THE VILLAINS STOLE MY PANTS!
AH... AFTER ALL, THEY ARE THIEVES, PANCHO!
BUT THEY DID NOT TAKE OUR DREAM. I STILL HAVE THAT!
OH MASTER YOU ARE TOO NOBLE FOR THIS WORLD.
LOOK... HERE COMES OUR TOWNSMAN, ALONZO QUIXANO
HE'S BEATEN UP BADLY! HE CALLS HIMSELF DON QUIXOTE NOW!
AS FELLOW TOWNFOLK WE MUST HELP HIM!
POOR MAN, HIS DREAMS WILL KILL HIM ONE DAY.
LET'S TALK TO SANCHO HIS - ER - SQUIRE
SANCHO, YOU MUST MAKE YOUR MASTER FACE REALITY!
KNIGHTHOOD IS IN THE PAST!
ALONZO IS NOT A REAL KNIGHT!
REST NOW SIRE - WHILE I TALK TO OUR TOWNFOLK... THEY'RE WORRIED.

WELL DID YOU TALK SENSE TO HIM?
SURELY SANCHO YOU SHOWED HIM HIS FOLLY?
NO...
NO?
NO?
I HAVE FELT THE POWER AND GLORY OF HIS DREAM!
I NOW BELIEVE HE IS DON QUIXOTE AND I AM HIS SQUIRE!
OOH
MASTER, WHAT ARE YOU DOING?
I AM NOW READY TO WED FAIR DULCINEA!
HERE IS MY LETTER TO HER...FIND HER, SANCHO!
Y-Y-YES... SIRE.

AT LAST ALL MY GOOD DEEDS MADE ME WORTHY OF HER!
OH... WHERE SHALL I FIND HER!
HOO...THAT LOOKS LIKE HER.
?
TRULY, SHE IS BEAUTIFUL! IT IS INDEED FAIR DULCINEA...
WELL, FAT-BOY... WHAT ARE YOU STARING AT??
HERE TAKE THIS LETTER FAIR BEAUTY, I'LL BE BACK...
BUT I CAN'T READ.

MASTER... I'VE **FOUND** THE FAIR **DULCINEA**... ... COME
I WILL BE IN MY ARMOR TO PRESENT MYSELF.
HURRY, SIRE!
THERE SHE IS, SIRE!
OH FAIR DULCINEA... HERE IS YOUR KNIGHT.
YOU TRYING TO MAKE A FOOL OF ME?
YOU BOOB! I AM **NOT** YOUR DULCINEA - OR WHOEVER!
SHE IS BEAUTIFUL, IS SHE NOT SIRE?
LET GO!

CALMLY, MY DEAR SANCHO.
IDIOTS!!
SHE IS ONLY A WINE SELLER.
BUT... I SAW HER BEAUTY ...I TRULY DID.
AHHH I SEE IT NOW... I HAVE BEEN DREAMING ..DREAMING!
IT WAS HER.. MAYBE SHE'S BE-WITCHED
NO, MY GOOD SANCHO YOU HAVE CAUGHT THE DREAM
BUT IT IS A GOOD DREAM, SIRE!
I DREAMED OF DOING GOOD DEEDS!!
AND SO YOU DID!
I DREAMED OF BEING A NOBLE KNIGHT.
AND SO YOU ARE.

A DREAM IS MOTHER TO THE DEED.
WELL-SAID.... SANCHO.
AND DEEDS ARE THE BRICKS OF LIFE!
AH WHAT GREAT WISDOM, SIRE.
BUT NOW I RETURN TO REALITY!
WAIT, MASTER... LOOK!
A WAGON... WITH A CAGED WILD LION!
I AM NO LONGER A KNIGHT!
NAY... I BELIEVE YOUR BRAVERY WAS NOT JUST A DREAM!
... GO FORTH BRAVE KNIGHT AND CHALLENGE THE BEAST!

I AM DON QUIXOTE I WOULD DO BATTLE WITH YOUR LION!
?
OUT OF OUR WAY, OLD FOOL!
Y'R CRAZY!!! THIS BEAST IS HUNGRY.
NUT!
I MUST GET HIM TO THE DUKE'S CASTLE, TONIGHT!
NO! RELEASE HIM, I SAY!
HE'LL TEAR YOU TO BITS!
VERY WELL, OPEN THE CAGE!
I'M SCARED.
ROAR

I'M GETTING OUT OF HERE.
ME TOO!

KEEP OUT OF THE WAY!
OOOH, THAT LION HAS NOT EATEN ALL DAY...OOH!
I AM READY FOR YOU, BEAST!
I AM ONLY ALONZO NOW!!
I FIGHT YOU AS A REAL MAN
TO SAVE MANKIND FROM YOUR CLAWS!
GRRR

YAWN
OHMY MASTER, HE'S **ASLEEP**!
?
?
ZZZ
TRUE THE LION DID FALL ASLEEP... BUT HE 'FACED' HIM ANYHOW.
AH WHAT BRAVERY
A TRUE KNIGHT!
WE MUST TELL THE COUNTRYSIDE ..YES, KNIGHTHOOD STILL FLOURISHES!
HAW... IS THAT ALL...HE DEFEATED A SLEEPY LION?
WELL THAT DID **BEGIN** THE LEGEND.
THE STORIES OF DON QUIXOTE'S ADVENTURES WERE WRITTEN INTO BOOKS.

SO?? HE HAD MANY MORE ADVENTURES THAN THE ONES YOU TOLD ME?
OH, YES! THEY ARE VERY FAMOUS.
BUT WHEN HE GREW OLD AND WAS DYING - DID HE STILL BELIEVE?
WELL... SADLY, NO! IN HIS LAST HOURS HE CALLED ME...
SANCHO... I NEVER WAS DON QUIXOTE... ALAS, I DIE ALONZO THE OLD FOOL.
NO, NO, NO... MASTER YOU ARE WHAT YOU BELIEVED! ... YOU GAVE US A DREAM!
YOU ENRICHED US BY YOUR VALOR! ... WE SAW REAL CHIVALRY.
AH SANCHO MY NEST OF DREAMS IS NOW EMPTY...
NO! THE BIRDS MAY HAVE FLOWN BUT THE DREAM REMAINS!!

WHO ARE YOU?
I'M MIGUEL DE CERVANTES THE AUTHOR

I HAVE WRITTEN A BOOK OF YOUR ADVENTURES... IT WILL BE READ FAR AND WIDE.

...YOUR DEEDS WILL SHOW PEOPLE THE VALUE OF DREAMS AND DREAMERS!

AND IT WILL BE KNOWN FOREVER THAT A CERTAIN ALONZO LIVED A DREAM
AHHH CERVANTES BELIEVES IN ME!

AND FROM THIS DREAM WAS BORN A GREAT KNIGHT... HE TO LIVE IT... AND ME TO WRITE ABOUT IT.

THEREFORE, I DUB THEE DON QUIXOTE DE LA MANCHA FOREVER!!

A KNIGHT WHO TRULY BELIEVES IN HELPING THE HELPLESS
AND LONG AFTER KNIGHTHOOD PASSED INTO HISTORY HE BECAME THE LAST KNIGHT.
AND SO HE DIED.
A HERO!
HONORED BY THE GREAT AUTHOR MIGUEL CERVANTES... READ BY MILLIONS OVER MANY GENERATIONS.
AHH...THAT WAS MANY, MANY YEARS AGO... DID QUIXOTE REALLY LIVE ??
IT DOESN'T MATTER... MAYBE HE DID AND MAYBE HE DIDN'T... BUT WHAT IS MOST IMPORTANT IS THAT HIS DREAM SURELY DID!